Frog's Snowy Day

Written by Suzanne Weyn
Illustrated by John Nez

MARVEL BOOKS

Flip the Frog awoke from a long winter's sleep.
"Since I'm awake, it must be the first day of spring," he
said with a yawn. "Time to get up."

Sleepily, he trudged to his front door and looked out. "Hmmmmm," he muttered. "I must be mistaken. This certainly doesn't look like spring to me."

Just then, a tiny mouse walked by. "Excuse me," called Flip to the mouse. "What day is it? And what is this strange white stuff?" Since Flip slept all winter, he had never seen snow before.

"It's the first day of spring," the mouse answered, "and this is snow. It's the last bit of winter, still hanging on."

"My name is Mac," said the mouse. "Why don't you come out to play with me? The snow is fun but it will soon be gone."

"No, no," said Flip, shutting the door. "I don't think I like snow. It's too strange." Flip decided he would much rather just go back to bed.

Flip was almost asleep when he heard a knock on his door. "What now?" he grumbled. He wrapped a tablecloth around his shoulders to keep warm and opened the door again.

"Ta da!" cried Mac the Mouse. "Come see what I made with snow!"

"That *is* quite nice," Flip agreed.

"Maybe I *would* like to see more of this snow," Flip said, "but my toes are so cold."

"Put these on your feet and you'll be just fine," said Mac.

Mac took Flip sledding. "Wheee!" they yelled as they raced down the hill.

Next, Mac taught Flip to ski.

Suddenly it began to snow. "Run for your life!" yelled Flip.

"Don't be scared," Mac said. "The snow comes from the sky, just like rain. See how pretty the flakes are."

"Oh," said Flip, and he caught a snowflake on his tongue.

Mac and Flip laughed as they threw snowballs at
each other. "Snow *is* wonderful!" cried Flip.

Mac tried to teach Flip to skate on his long, wobbly legs.

"Hee, hee," giggled Mac. "Maybe skating isn't for you."

"Hmmmph," said Flip, who didn't like falling and who liked being giggled at even less.

"Watch me," said Mac, skating out further onto the ice. But as Mac whirled round and round, Flip heard a rumble. Then a huge crack split through the ice.

"Help, I can't swim!" cried Mac as he tumbled into the cold water below the ice.

Quick as a flash, Flip dove into the water. "I'm coming, Mac!" he yelled.

He pulled Mac onto his back and swam with him to safety.

"Wake up, Mac. Please, wake up," said Flip.

At that moment, a ray of warm spring sun fell on Mac and Flip. Mac's eyes fluttered open and he looked up at his friend. "Gee, thanks," he said with smile. Flip smiled back at him happily.

"See, I told you spring was coming," said Mac. "The ice is melting."

"And the geese are returning from their winter vacation in the south," Flip pointed out.

'That's a sure sign of spring," said Mac.

Mac and Flip wandered about and watched the sun melt the snow. "Welcome spring! Welcome spring!" they sang happily.

And what a wonderful spring it was!